YOU AND ME

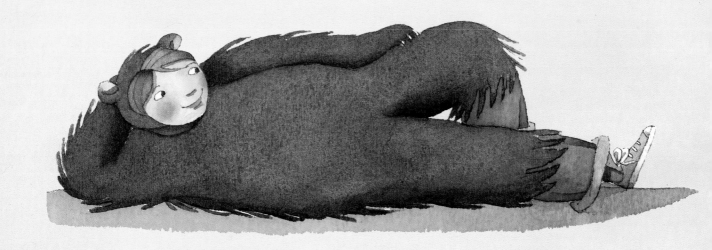

Barefoot Books
37 West 17th Street
4th Floor East
New York, New York 10011

This book is printed on 100% acid-free paper

This book was typeset in Infant Tekton 28pt
The illustrations were prepared in china ink on watercolor

Graphic design by Design/Section, England
Color separation by Grafiscan, Italy
Printed and bound in Hong Kong by South China Printing Co. (1988) Ltd.

1 3 5 7 9 8 6 4 2

U.S. Cataloging-in-Publication Data (Library of Congress Standards)

Blackstone, Stella.
    You and me / Stella Blackstone ; Giovanni Manna.-1st ed.
[32]p. : col. ill. ; cm.
Summary: A little boy and girl play a game of imagination, exploring
opposites and comparisons in the world around them.
ISBN 1-84148-263-3
1. Opposites -- Fiction. I. Manna, Giovanni, ill. II. Title.
[E] 21 2000 AC CIP

YOU AND ME

Giovanni Manna

walk
the way of wonder...
Barefoot Books

I'm a circle

You're a square

You're a tiger

I'm a bear

I'm a valley

You're a hill

You're moving

I'm still

I'm wild

You're tame

You're sunshine

I'm rain

I'm a tree